Candace

THE WATER-BUFFALO
CHILDREN

THE DRAGON FISH

To Candace
with love
from
Sylvia

June 29, 1967
"The Homestead"
Seattle, Washington

PEARL S. BUCK

THE WATER-BUFFALO CHILDREN

ILLUSTRATED BY WILLIAM A. SMITH

THE DRAGON FISH

ILLUSTRATED BY ESTHER BROCK BIRD

A YEARLING BOOK

Published by Dell Publishing Co., Inc.
750 Third Avenue, New York, N. Y. 10017
THE WATER-BUFFALO CHILDREN: Copyright © 1943 by Pearl S. Buck
THE DRAGON FISH: Copyright © 1944 by Pearl S. Buck
All rights reserved.
Published by arrangement with the original publisher,
The John Day Company, Inc.
First Dell printing—October 1966.
Printed in U. S. A.

Contents

THE WATER-BUFFALO CHILDREN

THE DRAGON FISH

THE
WATER-BUFFALO
CHILDREN

THE WATER-BUFFALO CHILDREN

"Did you have to speak Chinese?" Michael asked Mother. His eyes grew round.

"Certainly I did," Mother said. "When I was a little girl I lived in China where all the children speak Chinese."

"Do they mind?" Peter asked.

"Certainly not," Mother said. "They think it is the way to talk, just as you think your way is the way to talk. They feel very sorry for you, having to speak English."

The four children were sitting at the dinner table and the reason they were talking about China was that their mother had surprised them.

It was Saturday. They had played outdoors all morning doing only the things they liked to do. Just when they were thinking what to do next and just when David had said, "I am getting hungry," the big bell that hung on the porch began to clang.

Clangety-clang-clangety-clang! They knew when that big bell rang it meant "come home right away." So they hurried as fast as they could. There was Mother on the porch, and there was Daddy, smoking his pipe.

"There's a surprise!" Daddy called.

In exactly three minutes and a half, for Daddy timed them with his watch, they were washed and ready.

"Shut your eyes," Daddy said.

So they shut their eyes.

"Hold hands," Mother said.

8

Daddy took Peter's hand, for Peter is the oldest, and Mother took Judy's hand, for Judy is the youngest, and Michael and David were the be-tweens. They all marched to the dining room.

"Open your eyes!" Daddy said.

So they all opened their eyes and saw—the surprise. It was on the table. It was a Chinese dinner!

"How queer!" Judy said.

"It isn't really queer," Daddy said. "It's very good."

In the middle of the table were five bowls of food, all steaming hot, and at each place was a bowl of flaky dry rice, steaming hot.

"Everybody has rice at a Chinese dinner," Mother said.

"There are no knives and forks," David said.

"There are chopsticks," Mother said.

So that was the surprise, and everybody sat down, and they all learned how to hold their chop-sticks in one hand and their bowls in the other.

At first they were not sure they liked all the new tastes. But after one bite and two and three, they decided they did like them, and it was fun to eat with chopsticks. Then Mother began to tell them the Chinese names of all the dishes, and then Michael asked how Mother knew those names and then she said, "Because when I was a little girl I lived in China and played with Chinese children and talked Chinese."

"Which Chinese children did you like best?" Judy asked.

Mother had to think hard to answer that. "Well," she said at last, "next to the Chinese Children Next Door, I think I liked best the Water-Buffalo Children. They were brother and sister."

At this the children put down their chopsticks, since they were really very full.

"Tell us about the Water-Buffalo Boy," Michael said.

"No, tell us about his sister," Judy said.

"I'd rather hear about the Water-Buffalo," said Peter, who likes animals.

"What *is* a Water-Buffalo?" David asked.

"I'll tell you about all of them," Mother said. "But perhaps I had better begin with the Water-Buffalo, because I saw her first."

So she began with the Water-Buffalo.

"You must know, children," she said, "that the Water-Buffalo is a very strange beast. She looks like a cow because she is shaped like a very big cow, but she isn't a cow."

"Why not?" asked David.

"Because her horns are too wide and long," Mother said, "much wider and longer than a cow's horns. That's the first reason. She hasn't a skin like a cow, either, but much more like a rhinoceros, thick and black and without much hair, and that's the second reason she isn't like a cow. And she is called a Water-Buffalo because she

12

likes to get right under the water like a hippopota-
mus, and that's the third reason she isn't like a
cow. And I suppose there is a fourth reason, and it
is that though she can give a little milk if she has
to, she isn't used for milk but to pull plows for
farmers."

"Plows!" Peter cried. Peter knows all about
farming things because he likes farming. "Why,
that's funny!"

"If you lived in China you wouldn't think it was
funny," Mother said, "because almost everybody
plows with Water-Buffaloes there. Now this Water-Buffalo was called Big Turnip—"

The children burst out laughing. "Turnip!"
they cried—"Big Turnip!"

"Because she was so very slow," Mother said.
"It is not strange for a Water-Buffalo to be slow
for they are all slow. They would all rather stand
still than walk and they would rather soak themselves under water than anything else. But Big

Turnip was the slowest of all slow Water-Buffa-loes. The farmer to whom she belonged was Mr. Ching. He called her Big Turnip because she was so slow that she made him angry, and Big Turnip —well, it's what you call things in China that make you angry."

"Like dumb-bell," Peter said quickly.

"Exactly," Mother said. "Only of course the sound of Big Turnip was not that—in Chinese it is Da Lobo. So the Water-Buffalo was called Da Lobo, for Da is big and Lobo is turnip."

Here she had to stop for all the children to try saying "Da Lobo," which they did over and over, giggling, and Peter said, "What if I call a boy in school I don't like Da Lobo, Mother?"

"We had better go on with the story," Mother said quickly. So she went on.

"Now I can remember very well the very first day I ever saw Da Lobo. I had done my lessons early and my mother was a very busy woman and

15

so I ran outside the gate with my story book and
some peanuts so I wouldn't be under her feet, and
I made a nest for myself in the high pampas grass
outside the gate. The grass was so high that it was
over my head, and I tramped down a nice round
spot and when I sat down I could see out but nobody could see me. Then I opened the story book.
It was 'Arabian Nights,' I remember, because I
had just got to the story of Aladdin's lamp, and I
cracked my peanuts, and I was having a beautiful

time. The sun shone down into my little nest so warmly, I remember, and the crushed grass had a sweet smell under me, and far away in the valley a thrush sang a loud clear song. There was no wind, and it was a day in spring, not too hot and not too cold, and I remember feeling perfectly happy."

"I know that kind of a day," Judy said. "We have them here too."

"We do," Mother said. "Well, it *was* that kind of a day. I felt very good inside, I remember, for I

17

had done my lessons well that morning, and I had all the afternoon just for myself. So I kept on reading and eating peanuts and I came to the place where Aladdin rubbed his lamp, and I read on and he found the princess and I read on to the end of the story when they all lived happily ever after. When I finished the story I didn't feel like starting another right away. I lay on my back looking into the sky and thinking, 'What if I had a magic lamp?' I sat up and looked around me in the pampas grass. What if I found an old rusty magic lamp? Sometimes I did find strange things on the Chinese hills. There were old graves on them, made long ago, which people had forgotten, and the wind blew on them and the rains soaked them and sometimes the sides wore away, and I found old jars and bowls in them, that the long ago people had put there as we put flowers now. These jars I dug out and washed and kept in what I called my museum. Well, I looked around me that

18

day in the pampas grass, but I didn't see anything strange except a small very pretty white polished stone. It was an unusual stone to find there, where the land had few stones anyway. I picked it up and thought, 'What if this is a magic stone?' I held it a while and the longer I held it the more I felt perhaps it was a magic stone. So when I began to feel quite sure, I rubbed it as Aladdin rubbed the lamp —you remember?"

The children nodded. They knew all about Aladdin.

"And what happened?" David whispered. His blue eyes were very big.

"Nothing, the first time," Mother said. "So I held it a little while more to warm it up, and then I said 'Abracadabra!' just for good measure and I rubbed the stone hard, and then—"

Mother looked around at their faces. Even Daddy had taken his pipe out of his mouth and was listening.

"Something did happen," Mother said. "The tall pampas grass began to move, and I stooped and looked through the green stalks and I saw legs and four black hooves and a thin swishing tail, and I began to be a little scared. But what could I do except to sit still and wait? In a minute the legs were near, and the four hoofs came close, and I looked up and there above me was the big head, with wide black horns, of a Water-Buffalo! She had a big ring in her black nose, and there was a rope in the ring and it was wound around her neck. I jumped up, really afraid now, at what had come out of the stone, and I shrank back from the big face, and the big black eyes as big as tennis balls, and the great horns.

" 'Oh dear,' I cried, 'I wish I hadn't!'

"Then I saw what I hadn't seen before. On the back of the big Water-Buffalo were two children, one a boy about my age, and I was eight, and a little girl not bigger than five. They stared at me, and I stared at them, and pretty soon I saw they were as afraid of me as I was afraid of the Water-Buffalo, and so I wasn't afraid any more. At last the boy felt brave enough to speak first.

" 'Are you the foreign girl that lives in the house on top of the hill?' he asked me."

"Why did he call you foreign?" Michael asked.

"Because I was foreign to him," Mother said. "He was a Chinese boy in China, and he had black hair and black eyes, as all the Chinese have, and I was an American child living in China, and I had blue eyes and yellow hair, which he thought very funny."

"But we aren't funny, are we?" asked Michael, who has yellow hair himself.

"We are if we're in China," Mother said. "But I was used to that and I didn't mind it. So I said, 'Who are you?'

" 'I am Big Brother,' he said, 'and this is Little Sister, and the Buffalo is Da Lobo.'

"I laughed, just as you did, at the idea of calling a Water-Buffalo Big Turnip, and so I said, 'Why is the Water-Buffalo's name Da Lobo?'

" 'Because she is so slow she makes my father angry,' Big Brother said.

"All this time Little Sister had been holding him tight around his bare waist with her clasped arms, and she had not said one word.

"But she was a very pretty little girl. She had a round face and a small red mouth which she kept open all the time so you could see her teeth that were as white as rice, and her black hair was braided in one braid with a piece of scarlet yarn threaded through the braid, and she wore straight black bangs almost down to her round black eyes. Both she and Big Brother were barefoot, and Da

23

Lobo's back was so wide that their legs stuck straight out.

"Da Lobo, seeing that we had begun to talk, took the chance to stand still and do nothing, as she always did if she could. She rolled her eyes around to see what there was to eat, and chewed on the nearest pampas grass, although it was so tough and its edges so sharp that nothing but a Water-Buffalo could have eaten it.

" 'Come down,' I said to the two children. 'Let's play.'

"So Big Brother slid down, and when he slid Little Sister slid, too, for she did not let go of him for one minute, and when they both reached the ground she stood with her arms still tightly around his waist and peeping at me over his shoulder.

" 'Why is she afraid of me?' I asked Big Brother.

" 'How should I know?' Big Brother said. 'She's only a girl.'

" 'I am a girl, too,' I said, 'and I am not afraid.

At least I was only afraid for a minute of Da Lobo because I thought she had come out of my magic lamp—I mean my magic stone.'

" 'Where is your magic stone?' Big Brother asked.

"I picked up the white stone then. I had thrown it down when I was frightened of Da Lobo, and I held it out in my hand for him to see.

" 'Is it really a magic stone?' Big Brother asked, staring at it hard.

" 'When I rubbed it Da Lobo came with you on her back,' I said.

" 'But we were coming anyway,' Big Brother said. 'We were on our way to the other side of the hill to graze there. Father finished the rice plowing this morning and so he told me to take Da Lobo out to grass this afternoon, and to take her somewhere to find good new grass, so that was why we came this way.'

" 'Maybe the stone isn't magic,' I said.

" 'You rub it,' Big Brother said.

" 'No, you rub it,' I said.

"We were both a little afraid to rub it.

" 'You ought to rub it,' I said at last, 'because you're a boy.'

"Of course then Big Brother had to show that he was brave and he stepped forward and Little Sister clinging to his waist stepped forward too and when he found her still there he grew cross with her.

" 'Let go, you little rabbit," he said, and pulled her arms off his waist so that she began to cry.

" 'Don't call her a rabbit,' I said, for you must know that in China you don't call people rabbits because it is not nice, and when I saw poor Little Sister standing there with her big eyes full of tears, I felt so sorry I went and put my arms around her.

" 'You are *not* a rabbit,' I said, 'and he *is* a turtle.'

"This was naughty of me, for in China it is just

as bad to call people turtles as it is to call them rabbits.

" 'I am not a turtle,' Big Brother said.

" 'Then Little Sister is not a rabbit,' I said.

"He thought about this a minute, but he really was anxious to try the stone, and so he said,

" 'Let's not talk about rabbits and turtles,' and he picked up the stone, and rubbed it a very little. Nothing happened.

" 'You have to say "Abracadabra",' I said.

" 'What is that?' he asked astonished.

" 'It's a magic word,' I said.

" 'If it's foreign magic I won't say it,' he said.

" 'It's not foreign magic, it's just magic,' I told him. 'See, I will write it for you,' and I took a stick and smoothed a place on the hard ground and scratched the word on it as plainly as I could.

" 'I can't read,' he said. 'I never went to school. But those letters don't look right to me. I never saw any like them. They must be foreign letters. I would rather not say it.'

" 'Then the stone won't do its magic for you.' I told him.

"He thought a while about this and then he said, 'I'll take the stone home and keep it over night and if I dare to say it tomorrow I'll come back here when the sun is half way between the hill and the top of the sky,' and he pointed his finger to the spot.

" 'What if you still don't dare?' I asked.

" 'Then I'll come back and tell you so,' he said, 'and I'll give you back the stone.'

"So he put the stone inside his girdle, for he only wore short pants and his girdle was a strip of blue cloth wrapped around his waist and he used it for pockets as well as to keep his pants up. Then he shouted at Da Lobo who all this time had been standing very still, chewing the grass and not liking it very well as you could see from the tired look in her eyes, but still she kept on chewing it instead of moving along to anything better, because she was very lazy. But when Big Brother shouted she obeyed him like a lamb, although she was a huge beast and he only a small boy.

" 'Down!' he shouted.

"At the sound of his voice she put down her head and he leaped on it, holding himself by her great horns, and he crawled up her neck and in a minute, a second, much quicker than I can tell you about it, he was on her back again with his legs sticking straight out. Then Little Sister took hold of Da Lobo's stringy tail and climbed

 up her back legs just as briskly and sat herself behind him with her legs stick- ing straight out.

" 'Until we meet,' they both said, which is the way you say good-bye in Chinese.

" 'Until we meet tomorrow,' I said.

"Da Lobo knew of course that now she must move but she didn't until the very last minute she had to, and that minute was when Little Sister turned round and twisted her tail hard. Then Da Lobo blew air through her big nose, and very slowly she moved her big body and soon all I could see were the two dark heads of Big Brother and Little Sister above the tall pampas grass."

Here Mother stopped to remember and to smile, because she forgot where she was. Whenever Mother did this the children wanted her to come back to them quickly out of what she was remembering, which was so far away.

"Mother, Mother!" Judy cried.

Peter slipped out of his chair and came running around the table to lean against Mother.

"Don't stop, Mother," Michael said.

"*Was* it a magic stone?" David asked.

"How did I know?" Mother said. "I couldn't decide, myself, even when I went home. I didn't tell anybody, because if you tell about magic things they aren't magic any more. In the night when I woke up and heard the big bell in the temple boom through the darkness I thought about the stone and it seemed to me then that it must be magic. But I was always a little afraid of the sound of the bell in the night. That bell had thunder in it. I had been in the temple and stood near it when a priest struck it and the sound was louder than thunder. At night, alone in my bed, I could feel it rolling up the hill like thunder."

"I'm afraid of thunder," Peter said in such a small voice that Mother gave him a squeeze.

"I used to be afraid of thunder, too," she said, "and maybe that is why the big bell always scared me a little. So that night when I heard it I was sure the stone was magic. But when I got up in the morning and ate a big dish of porridge just as I always did, and saw the sun shining everywhere around, I wasn't so sure about the magic.

"I hurried through my lessons that day, I remember, though I had three times three to learn and usually I was slow at multiplication tables. My mother was so surprised that she asked me what I was going to do after my lessons and she hoped it wasn't anything naughty that made me so quick.

" 'Oh no, it's not naughty,' I said. 'It's only

something magic but I can't tell you about it until afterward.'

"So when the sun was exactly half way between the hill and the top of the sky and exactly at the spot where Big Brother's finger had pointed yesterday, I was in my nest in the pampas grass waiting. I didn't have to wait long. In a very few minutes I saw the two heads bobbing over the top of the tall grass, and in a minute more the grass parted and there was Da Lobo again, looking exactly as she had yesterday, but today I wasn't

afraid of her. And there, too, on her back, was Big Brother in his short blue cotton pants, and I could see the stone bulging in his girdle, and behind him was Little Sister in her little faded red jacket and blue pants, and she was clutching him around the waist, and their bare legs were sticking out. But Big Brother looked very solemn.

" 'Big Brother and Little Sister,' I said, 'have you eaten your rice?' "

"Why did you ask that?" David asked Mother.

"Because," Mother said, "that is the polite way in China to say, 'How do you do?'

"Big Brother was polite, too.

" 'I have eaten,' he said. 'Have you?'

" 'I have,' I said.

"Little Sister was not so shy today, and at this moment she piped up. 'But you don't eat rice,' she said. 'You are a foreigner and you eat rats and dogs and cow's fat.'

" 'I do not,' I said. 'Whoever told you such lies?'

" 'That's what we've always heard about foreigners,' Big Brother said.

" 'I eat just what you eat,' I said. 'I eat rice and meat and vegetables.'

" 'But you do eat cow's milk and cow's fat,' Little Sister said.

" 'It's not cow's fat—it's butter,' I said, 'and it is good, especially on bread.'

" 'I wouldn't eat it,' Little Sister said. 'I'd be afraid it would make me smell.'

" 'If you go on talking like that,' I said to Little Sister, 'I shall be sorry I wouldn't let Big Brother call you a rabbit yesterday.'

"At this Little Sister shut her red mouth and stared at me very hard, and Big Brother turned around and pretended to slap her.

" 'You have no manners,' he said to her. 'What will this foreign girl think of you?'

" 'That's all right,' I said, trying to be nice. 'She's very small.'

37

" 'Yes, she is,' Big Brother said, 'and besides she is only a girl.'

" 'But I told you I am a girl,' I cried when he said this again.

" 'You mustn't mind me,' Big Brother said quickly. 'I have no manners either. Besides, you don't look like a girl. You are so big.'

"Now I saw he was trying to be nice and so we all forgave each other, and Da Lobo stood perfectly still as she always did when she had a chance and chewed pampas grass with a tired look because she didn't like it any better today than she had yesterday.

" 'This stone,' Big Brother said, taking the white stone out of his girdle, 'is a magic stone. I have decided that.'

" 'Why do you think it is?' I asked.

" 'Because,' he said, 'it is so white that in the night it could be seen on the table near my bed. And my father saw it when he came in and he said,

"What is that so white on the table?" and I said, "It is a stone." And he lit the candle and took the stone in his hand and he said, "It *is* a strange stone. I never saw such a smooth white stone. Don't lose it." Even he thought it was strange so it must be magic.'

" 'Then do you want to say "Abracadabra" to-day?' I asked him.

" 'I will rub the stone,' he said, 'and you say that word.'

"So that was what we did. I said 'Abracadabra' three times very slowly and he rubbed the stone, while Little Sister held on tight and shut her eyes."

"What happened?" Michael whispered.

"Nothing," Mother said, "nothing at all, though we all waited. A bee flew out of the grass, a big yellow and black bumble bee, but that was nothing. A little green snake slithered out and saw us and slithered away again, but that was nothing. Little Sister opened her eyes at last and all the time Da Lobo had not stopped chewing.

" 'It doesn't work that way,' I told Big Brother when we had waited a long time. 'The same person has to rub and say "Abracadabra" or the genie won't come.'

" 'Then you do it,' he said, holding out the stone to me.

" 'If I do you won't get your wish,' I said.

" 'I'll tell you what I want,' he said quickly. 'I want—'

" 'No, don't tell me,' I cried out. 'If you tell your wish you won't get it.'

"Now we were in a predicament.

" 'Predicament' is a long hard word, because a predicament is hard to get out of.

"What could we do? At last Big Brother set his teeth and screwed up his round brown face.

" 'I'll say it,' he said, holding the stone in both hands. 'I'll say it and rub at the same time.'

"Then he thought of something. 'What if Da

Lobo is frightened and runs when the genie comes?'

" 'Da Lobo can't run,' I said laughing.

" 'Yes, she can,' Little Sister piped out. 'The first time she saw a white man she ran four miles into the next province.'

" 'Yes, she did,' Big Brother said. 'She can run very fast when she's scared.'

"Here was another predicament.

"What would we do if Da Lobo did run? She would run away with Big Brother and Little Sister and leave me standing there with the genie and no wish ready.

" 'I don't want to be left here all alone,' I said.

" 'You get on Da Lobo, too,' Big Brother said quickly. 'There is plenty of room. My older brother used to sit on her with us before he got married. You can sit between us so you won't fall off.'

"It seemed a good idea. He slid down over Da Lobo's head, and held her by the ring in her nose while I tried to climb up. But Da Lobo didn't like the idea of my sitting on her at all."

"Why not?" Judy asked.

"She was used to her own kind of children but  not to me," Mother said. "She tried to hold her head up high so I couldn't get on her, and she rolled her eyes around and spat out the pampas grass she was chewing.

"Big Brother beat her with his fists and called her a few names and then he wound the rope around his foot so she had to keep her head down and I climbed up and sat in the middle of her back and Little Sister put her arms around me.

" 'You do smell of milk,' she said sniffing, 'and you do smell of cow's fat!"

"I turned around and sniffed her. 'And you smell of garlic,' I said, 'garlic and pig's fat.'

" 'Do I?' she said. 'But that's what I had for dinner!'

"While we were talking Big Brother was unwinding the rope and tying it again around Da Lobo's neck where it usually was, and in a second he had climbed up her back and was in front of me, and I was clutching him around the waist. Da Lobo's back looked so broad, but it was really very slippery, and her backbone was sharp and it was hard to sit right on top of it. Besides, it was the very first time I had ever sat on top of a Water-Buffalo. It looks easier than it is."

Mother was laughing again and now so was Daddy.

"I can just see you," Daddy said, laughing.

They both looked
at each other
laughing and as
though they had
forgotten where
they were, re-
membering.

"But was the
stone magic?"
Peter asked, to bring them back again to here and
now.

"Well," Mother said, "I will let you decide. For
this is what happened. When we were all settled
except Da Lobo—"

"What was the matter with Da Lobo?" Peter
asked.

"She kept turning her long neck to stare at me,"
Mother said. "It seemed to me I saw a queer look
in her big black eyes. She looked as though she
were counting us. It seemed to me she was saying

45

to herself, 'Is it one—two up there, or is it one—two—three?'

" 'I don't think Da Lobo likes me to be here,' I told Big Brother.

" 'It is because you do smell of milk,' Little Sister said, 'and it makes her feel uncomfortable.'

"Da Lobo turned her big head up this way and looked at me and she turned it up that way and looked at me, and each time she turned, one of her horns stuck into my thigh a little because her horns were very long and being in the middle I was just in the right place to be poked by them when she turned her head.

"Big Brother reached down for the rope and unwound it again.

" 'Da Lobo,' he shouted, 'your mother and grandmother were accursed!' And as he said this he pulled the rope so hard that Da Lobo shivered her skin and we nearly all slipped off.

" 'She does that when she doesn't want us on her

46

back,' Little Sister said.

" 'Let's hurry up and try the magic stone and then if nothing happens I'll get off,' I said. So Big Brother took the stone and rubbed it and repeated after me 'Abracadabra'."

"What happened?" Michael whispered.

"Well," Mother said, "nothing, because you see he couldn't say it just right. He said 'Ablacadabla,' because 'r' was hard for Chinese to say. I had to repeat it again and again, and I showed him how my tongue went against my teeth to make 'r,' and all the time Da Lobo was heaving her big round sides in and out so that we felt we were sitting on a folding thing like an accordion. Then suddenly Big Brother said it exactly right, and he rubbed the stone at the same time and—"

Mother paused and looked at the listening children. All the eyes were fixed on her face, even Daddy's.

"What did happen?" Judy whispered.

"Something happened," Mother said. "For the moment he shouted 'Abracadabra' just right and rubbed the stone, Da Lobo gave a great squeaky bellow and threw up her head and ran. How she ran! She ran through the pampas grass down the hill, over the rough places and over the smooth, and we clung to each other, and Little Sister shrieked and cried, and Big Brother pulled on the rope and shouted and cursed and we all hung on to each other and it was exactly like riding an earthquake. We bounced in the air and from side to side, and we dug in our heels and clung together, and barely didn't fall off. As for Da Lobo, nothing could stop her. She heaved and panted and ran, her head down, and the ring pulling her nose so that it must have hurt dreadfully. But she didn't care. She ran straight for the place she loved best and felt the safest in, and where do you suppose that was?"

Nobody could imagine and so nobody answered.

"It was in the big pond at the bottom of the hill." Mother said. "We saw her heading for it but we didn't dare to fall off because she was going so fast. We just held each other and shut our eyes and the next minute we were all in the pond, and

the muddy water was around our necks. We were still sitting on Da Lobo. We could feel her big quivering body under us, but all we could see of her was the black pad of her nose above the water, breathing in and out in big snorts.

"Of course everybody came running from the paddy fields to help us, and Big Brother's father

was the first to get there, and he waded in and picked us off, one by one. He was a very nice man, and he didn't scold at all. Instead when he had set us on the bank he asked,

" 'What under the sky made Da Lobo run? I never saw her run like that before.'

" 'It was the magic stone,' Big Brother faltered.

" 'What magic stone?' Mr. Ching asked. He was a farmer and he wore his work clothes, which were a pair of blue cotton pants, rolled around his bare knees, and his clean brown back was bare except for a strip of blue cloth he used to wipe his sweat away when he was hot. Now we had made him quite wet and so he wiped himself while he talked.

" 'That stone you saw on my table last night,' Big Brother said.

" 'Where is it?' Mr. Ching asked.

"Where was it? We looked at each other. 'I had it in my hand,' Big Brother said, 'when Da Lobo carried us all into the water.'

"He held out both his hands. They were empty.

" 'You must have dropped it,' said Mr. Ching. 'In that case it is lost in the mud at the bottom of the pond.'

"We looked at each other sadly. Now how would

we ever know whether that stone was magic or not?

" 'Da Lobo must have seen something,' Big Brother said. 'Because she never runs when she doesn't see anything.'

" 'Unless she is stung by a bee,' Mr. Ching said, looking at Da Lobo. She was still under water except her black nose.

" 'There was a bee,' I said doubtfully.

" 'Or it may have been a snake,' Mr. Ching said. 'Da Lobo hates snakes. I know when she feels one in the mud when we are plowing for rice she shakes all over and tries to lift her four feet at once.'

" 'There was a snake,' I said.

" 'Maybe she didn't like you,' Little Sister said cruelly to me. 'After all, you are a foreign girl and you do smell of milk.'

" 'Pei!' Mr. Ching cried quickly to her. 'How rude you are, Little Sister!' He sniffed me a little. 'I smell you are a little different from us, but it's a

nice smell,' he said to make me feel better.

"By now he had wiped himself dry. 'Now,' he said, 'you had better all go home and change your clothes.' Then he turned to the pond. 'Da Lobo!' he cried. 'Come out!' But Da Lobo would not come out. Her black nose only snorted.

"He picked up a bamboo stick that lay near by, for they kept it there to prod Da Lobo with when she did not want to come out of the pond and go to work, and he felt under the water and gave her two or three good digs. At this Da Lobo's head came up for one minute and she looked around.

56

Then she went down again so deep that not even
her nose showed. There were only a few bubbles.

"Mr. Ching gave up. 'Well, well,' he said, 'let her drown!' He didn't mean this because he knew Water-Buffaloes have to come up. They can't stay under water too long. But he said it loudly to show her he did not care, and he went home, and Big Brother and Little Sister went after him dripping, and I dripped my way up the hill. Every now and then I turned to see whether Da Lobo was still under water, and by the time I was at the top of the hill she was out and eating grass on the bank, and I saw Mr. Ching sneak up on her and grab the end of the rope and march her home again. Then I went in to change my clothes and tell my mother what had happened to me."

"What did she say?" Peter asked. He was interested because he is himself the kind of boy who is always falling in the water so that over and over again Mother had said, "Really, Peter, I don't know *what* to do with you."

"What did my mother say?" Mother repeated.

"Why, when she saw me standing there all dripping, she said, 'Really, child, I don't know what to do with you!'"

They all laughed at this and Daddy got up and lit his pipe.

"Good story," he said. "Wasn't it?" he asked the children.

None of them answered for a moment. It was Michael who spoke first. "But, Mother," he said, "*was* it a magic stone?"

Mother threw up her two hands. "How can I ever know?" she said. "Nobody knew except Da Lobo, and she couldn't tell!"

THE DRAGON FISH

ONCE UPON A TIME, but not
so long ago, there lived in the land of China a little girl
whose name was Lan-may. She was the only girl in this
Chinese family and she had three brothers. She was the
youngest child and she was eight years old. Her brothers were Sheng, Tsan, and Yung. Yung was nine years
old, while Tsan was ten and Sheng was thirteen.

They all lived together in a brick house that had a
tile roof, and the house was in a pretty green valley

near the great Yangtse River. Their father was a farmer, and some of the fields went straight down to the river's edge, and so he was a fisherman, too. His name was Mr. Wu. He had no time to fish because he had to farm, and so he put up a big four-cornered net, stretched on bamboos, and hung from a long bamboo pole. Anybody who had time ran down to the water's edge and pulled up a rope which pulled up the net. If there were any fish they wriggled in the bottom of the net and then were dipped up with a long-handled dipper. If there were no fish, then whoever pulled the rope let it loose again and the net sank back into the yellow waters of the river.

Of course there was Mrs. Wu. But she was a quiet woman who did not speak unless she was spoken to, and she was very busy with so many boys and Mr. Wu to feed and to mend for and take care of in many ways. She was so busy that she had very little time to talk with Lan-may. Sheng, Tsan, and Yung talked a great deal with their father when they came home from school and when they worked in the fields on holidays. But nobody seemed to talk very much with Lan-may. Sometimes Mr. Wu happened to see her and he would say, "Ah, is that you, Lan-may? Go and fetch me my pipe."

Or Sheng would say, "Lan-may, you have nothing to do. Bring me a bowl of tea."

Or Tsan would say, "Since you have nothing to do, Lan-may, you might feed the pig."

Or Yung would say, "Lan-may, you are only a girl, you must sweep the threshing floor."

Lan-may did all these things, and then wished that someone would talk to her, but no one ever did. She had a little black and white cat which she loved very much, and to which she talked a good deal, but all the cat could do was to purr, and that grew monotonous.

"I wish I were not the only girl," Lan-may said one day to her mother, who was quiet as usual. "If we had another girl, I would have someone to talk to, instead of always having to be quiet."

"It is good for little girls to be quiet," Mrs. Wu said. She was shelling broadbeans, and she did not look up when she spoke.

"Why?" Lan-may asked.

"Because then they will grow up to be quiet women," Mrs. Wu said.

"Why should they be quiet women?" Lan-may argued.

"So they won't bother men," Mrs. Wu said and put her lips together so firmly that Lan-may knew she would not talk any more.

"Couldn't we have another girl?" Lan-may asked her father when he came in that night from the fields.

"A girl?" Mr. Wu said in astonishment. "Why, what would we do with her?"

"I could play with her," Lan-may said.

"It is time for you to learn to work," Mr. Wu said, "so it is not worth while to get another girl." And he began to wash his hands and face in the tin basin that stood on a little table in the kitchen and so she knew he was not going to talk any more.

"I wish you were a girl," Lan-may said to Yung. Yung was a very mischievous teasing boy and he had just pulled her pigtail so hard that the tears came into her eyes.

"Me—a girl?" he shouted, and he laughed so long that she almost began to cry.

"Yes—yes—yes," she said, "I do wish it! I am so tired of boys!"

At that moment Sheng came into the house. He was in his best clothes because he was going to town to sell some eggs. "Lan-may," he said in a great hurry, "I forgot to see if there are any fish in the net. Please run to the river for me."

And Lan-may went. She had to obey Sheng because he was her older brother. "If I had a sister," she

thought, pouting as she walked, "we could go together and we would sit by the river and talk and throw little stones and talk some more and then I would never be lonely."

As if it were not enough she met Tsan on her way down to the river. He was coming in from the field and he had his hoe on his shoulder. "Lan-may," he cried, "come home and help me make a spear!"

"I don't want to make a spear," she said. "I am tired of spears and boys' things."

She hurried on quite alone. How nice it would be, she thought, if she had a girl to play with, so that they could play dolls and keeping house! As it was she had to play alone or else she had to play wars and battles and robbers with her brothers, and she was often very tired of that, especially because none of the boys would willingly be the enemy and so she had to be the enemy, and all of them wanted to be robbers and so she had always to be robbed, and when they played hide and seek she had always to be the seek.

By now she was down to the river's edge. There the great net hung deep in the running yellow water of the Yangtse River. She felt in no great hurry and so she did not pull it up at once. Instead she sat down on the thick soft grass that grew brightly green along the river's edge. She looked around. Everything was just the same as it was always. The river was very wide here and she could just see the green stripe of the land across the water. She wondered if that side were like this side and if the people over there were the same as they were here. She had heard that the people across wide waters were different—foreigners, they were called. She had never seen one, but she had listened to persons who had seen them, and it was like listening to fairy tales. The foreigners across the water, they had said, had pink skin instead of brown, and blue eyes or green eyes or gray eyes, instead of black ones, and sometimes their hair, instead of being black, was red and sometimes it was tawny as a lion's mane, and sometimes yellowish brown like a dog's fur. When they talked, she had heard, their language was so strange that no one could understand it. It was full of "k-k-k" and "ff-ff-ff" and "ss-ss-ss"—that was what the old cloth peddler had said who had once traveled to Shanghai on a boat to buy foreign cloth.

The sky was very blue above the yellow water, and she wondered about the foreign sky. Was it blue too, or was it perhaps green or purple or some such color?

"There is really no one to tell me anything," she thought sadly. "My mother is a quiet woman, and my father is a busy man, and my brothers are all boys."

When she thought of her father she remembered she had been sent here to the river to pull up the net. So she scrambled to her feet and took hold of the rough rope and began to pull it up. The net seemed very heavy and for a moment she was excited. Suppose there were a big fish in it, or even two or three? Should

she try to dip the fish up herself? Or should she run home and tell her father? And if she did this, what if the fish jumped out while she was gone?

The net grew more and more heavy as she pulled, until she was quite sure there was something unusual in it. Slowly it came out of the water, first the four corners stretched on bamboo poles, then the sides, and now the middle hung down as heavy as a bag.

"It must be an *enormous* fish!" she cried out loud, and now she really pulled as hard as she could, and at last the net was almost out of the water, and then it was out and she could see the bottom.

There was no big fish at all. Instead, at the bottom of the huge square net lay one little fish, quite still as though it were dead. Even its color was nothing unusual. It was only a dull brown.

"How can that fish weigh so much?" she thought. Of course she was very much disappointed, so much that she was about to let the net sink back into the river as her father did if there were only a little fish in it.

"I really must see why it weighs so much," she thought. So she tied the end of the rope firmly around a crooked post which her father had driven deep into the earth for just that purpose, and she reached for the dipper that was fastened on the end of a long bamboo pole, and holding one of the corner ropes of the net, she leaned over and slipped the dipper under the fish and tried to lift it out.

It was so heavy she could scarcely lift it. Now that the fish was in the dipper, the thin bamboo handle bent

when she tried to lift it.

She sat down on the bank and wondered what she ought to do. If she went back to her father, someone might come by and take the fish while she was gone. Then her father would think she had only had a silly dream. She leaned over as far as she dared and stared at the fish. It lay quite still as though it were dead. Perhaps it was dead. Perhaps she just ought to let the net down into the river again and see what happened.

Now it occurred to her that she need not lift the fish but just let the wooden dipper float on the water as she lowered the net and then she could pull it across the water to her. This she did, very carefully letting the rope go until the net was in the water again, but not too deeply, and as the dipper floated, she pulled it to her and so drew the fish to the shore. There the fish lay in the bottom of the dipper, quiet and still. Now that it was close she saw that it was no ordinary fish. It was shaped like a tiny dragon. It had four little feet on four short legs, instead of fins, and its tail was long and curling.

"It's a dragon fish," she thought and was quite excited. She had heard of dragon fish but she had never seen one before. Dragon fish, people said, brought good luck. But where was the good luck now? She looked

up at the sky—it was as quiet and blue as ever. She looked at the river, and its swift yellow waters were running along just as usual. She looked at the grass, and it was standing still and hot in the sunshine. But now she saw some little blue flowers that she had not seen before. And when she looked at the river she saw some wild ducks fly down and settle there, and when she looked up in the sky she saw a big white bird like a heron flying slowly across it, and of course a heron is another sign of good luck.

Now she was sure that something was about to happen. She stood up and gazed all around her. At that very moment she saw a girl walking along the edge of the river and coming toward her. She stood quite still with astonishment. For this girl was not an ordinary girl. Lan-may first noticed her dress. Lan-may wore a pink flowered short coat and trousers, and on her feet white socks and black sateen shoes which her mother made. Lan-may's hair was braided into two tight pigtails and tied with pink yarn, and in front it was cut into bangs. But this girl wore a skirted dress, gathered in front, short sleeved and very full, and it was made of blue linen. Her legs were bare except for short white socks and a pair of black leather low shoes. Her hair was floating about her face, but the strange thing about the hair was that it was yellow.

Lan-may was sure that this was some sort of a fairy who had come up out of the water, and she grew very much afraid. She wanted to run, but her feet seemed stuck to the ground—she could not move. She opened her mouth so that she could breathe more quickly because her heart was beating so fast. When the girl came nearer, Lan-may saw that her eyes were just as blue as her dress, and her skin was not brown but pinkish.

"I didn't take your dragon fish," Lan-may stammered. "It came up in the net. I only pulled it out."

"What dragon fish?" the girl asked. She was quite close now and Lan-may was terrified. Never had she seen a girl with blue eyes and yellow hair and pinkish skin!

Lan-may pointed down to the strange heavy little fish. "There it is," she said, "you may have it back."

The girl bent over and looked at the heavy little fish. "That's not my dragon fish," she said, "I never saw it before."

"Then whose is it?" Lan-may asked. "For I never saw it before. And look, it doesn't move—it just lies there."

The dragon fish had not moved at all.

"Pick it up," said the yellow-haired girl.

"I can't," Lan-may said. "It is so heavy."

19

"Then I'll pick it up," the yellow-haired girl said.

So she put out her pinkish hands and slipped them under the fish. "It is heavy," she said, "and, oh, how cold it is!"

Now that the girl had picked up the dragon fish, Lan-may did not feel afraid any more. "Let me have it," she said.

But the yellow-haired girl would not. "Maybe it is my fish," she said, "you said it was."

"You told me it wasn't!" Lan-may cried, "and, after all, it came up in my father's net."

They were quarreling, although they had never seen one another before, and so they both began to laugh.

"What is your name?" the yellow-haired girl asked.

"Lan-may," Lan-may replied.

"Mine is Alice," the girl said.

"Alish—" Lan-may could not say the strange name.

"Aliss-ss-ss," the girl said.

"Aliss-ss-ss," Lan-may echoed. "Why are you named Aliss-ss-ss?"

"Because my father and mother wanted to name me that," the girl said. "My two brothers are called Tom and Jack."

"I have three brothers," Lan-may said. "They are Sheng, Tsan, and Yung, and I am very tired of them."

"Are you?" Alice cried. "I am tired of Tom and Jack. And I wish I had a sister."

"Do you?" Lan-may cried. "I want a sister, too. But my mother says she is too busy for more girls."

"Does she? That is what my mother says."

The two little girls looked at one another and the same thought came to their lips at the same time. "Let's *us* be sisters. Yes, yes!" they shouted, and then they laughed together.

"I'll let you hold the fish," Alice said, "because you're my sister."

Lan-may held out her open hands and Alice put the fish into them. "It is heavy," Lan-may said, "and it is cold."

"It is not alive at all, I think," Alice said.

"It feels smooth like a real fish," Lan-may said. "But it is very hard. Yes, it must be dead."

"Let's scrape it just a little," Alice said. She took a bit of sharp stone and scraped the dragon fish a very little. Under the brownish slime which the river had put upon it, a green color shone through. "Why, it's a pretty fish," Alice said. "We must scrape it all clean."

They both began to scrape and to rub the dragon fish with sand, and in a few minutes it was shining bright and green. It was not alive after all. Now they could see it clearly. It was made of a bright green stuff as hard as stone. Somebody had made it and somehow it had been dropped into the river and somehow the strong river water had carried it into the net.

Just at this moment two voices floated through the air. One came from upstream, and it called very high and clear, "*Alice, Alice!*"

"That's my mother," Alice said hurriedly. "I have to go."

The second came from downstream, and it called very loud and clear, "Lan-may, *Lan-may!*"

"That's my father," Lan-may said hurriedly, "and I must go, too!"

"What shall we do with the fish?" Alice asked.

"What shall we do with it?" Lan-may echoed.

"Let's keep it for our secret," Alice said.

"Let's keep everything for our secret," Lan-may said eagerly. "Let's not tell anybody anything, especially our brothers."

"Oh, that would be fun," Alice cried.

"We'll bury the dragon fish," Lan-may said, "right here by these blue flowers. Then we'll remember where it is. When we come here again we'll dig it up and play with it, just you and I."

"Oh, yes," Alice cried. So they buried the fish be-

side the blue flowers, digging the sandy earth up with their fingers and then washing them again in the yellow river water. Then they stood up and looked at each other.

"Good-by, Sister," Alice said to Lan-may.

"Good-by, Sister," Lan-may said to Alice.

They put their arms about one another and each gave the other a big hug.

"Come back after you have eaten," Lan-may said.

"I will," Alice said, "and if I'm late you must wait for me."

"I will," Lan-may said, "and if I am late you must wait for me."

"I will," Alice promised.

Then they waved and ran a little way and waved again and ran home. And all the way home Lan-may was excited and happy. "I have a sister," she thought, "a real sister. She can't help it if she has yellow hair and blue eyes and pinkish skin and anyway she is a girl."

"Where have you been so long?" Lan-may's father asked a little crossly when she got home. They were all eating already, and he did not like anyone to be late.

"Wash your hands and face," Lan-may's mother said. "You are dirty."

So she went to wash her hands and face. "Where

24

were you, I say?" Mr. Wu asked again when she came back.

"At the river," she said. It was very hard to keep the secret.

"Were there no fish?" Mr. Wu asked.

"Only one little one," she said. She took up her chopsticks and began to eat very fast.

"Did you throw it back?" he asked.

Now Lan-may was not at all good at telling lies and so before she knew it she blurted out the truth. "I buried it," she said.

Mr. Wu was shocked. He put down his chopsticks. "Do you mean to tell me, my daughter, that you buried a small live fish that could have grown to be a big one?"

"It wasn't alive," Lan-may faltered.

"Ah then, that's different," Mr. Wu grumbled. "But even so you should have thrown it back for it could have been food for the other fish."

"It was a very hard fish," Lan-may faltered.

Mr. Wu had just picked up his chopsticks and now he put them down again.

"Hard?" he repeated. "What do you mean?"

"It was just—hard," Lan-may said in a small voice.

"You mean it wasn't a real fish?" Mr. Wu asked.

"I think it was made of stone," Lan-may said. "Any-

26

way, it was heavy."

At this Mr. Wu grew really excited. "But why didn't you bring it home?" he demanded. "Perhaps it was gold, or jade, or something precious. After all, such things have been found in the river. When we have eaten you must take me to where you buried it and we will see what this fish is."

"Yes, Father," Lan-may said in a small voice. She tried to eat but now she felt very badly. The dragon fish was to have been a secret. She had promised Alice not to tell. "The fish doesn't belong just to me," she told her father.

Mr. Wu was really cross at this. He put down a bit of chicken and said in a severe voice, "What do you mean now?"

"It is only half mine," she said. "The other half belongs to someone else."

"To whom?" Mr. Wu said in a loud voice. "Didn't it come up in our net?"

"Please, Father," said Lan-may, "I can't explain."

But Mr. Wu would not have this. He was a very determined man. Now his brushy eyebrows stood up and he made his eyes round as he said to Lan-may, "I insist—who is this other person?"

Lan-may hung her head and twisted her hands.

27

Everybody was looking at her in astonishment. Mrs. Wu, being quiet, said nothing as she looked, but the three boys began to wink and to laugh. Lan-may saw that she had to say something. "It belongs to my sister as well as to me," she said very quickly.

Now everybody was really astonished.

"Ho!" cried Sheng, "if you have a sister, I have a sister!"

"We all have a sister, if you have a sister," Tsan said.

And Yung cried, "I don't want another sister!"

"Wife," Mr. Wu said solemnly to Mrs. Wu, "do we have another daughter that you have never told me about?"

Mrs. Wu shook her head and said nothing. She had been quiet all her life and she went on being quiet.

But Lan-may began to cry. "Now you have made me tell my secret!" she said furiously. "And my sister doesn't want any more brothers. She has too many— just as I have. I don't want her brothers and she doesn't want mine. We are just sisters, that's all!"

And Lan-may was so angry that she jumped up from her stool and ran out of the house crying and down to the river. She dug up the earth beside the blue flowers and there the little green dragon fish was lying very still. When she saw it she felt quite happy again. After all, she had not told the whole secret. She had not told that her sister's name was Alice and that she had blue eyes and yellow hair. No, no, that she would never tell, for then Sheng and Tsan and Yung would laugh at poor Alice, who could not help looking so queer.

But now what would she do? Her father would come down to the river as soon as he had eaten, to find the fish, and the boys would come down to see it, and then they would take the fish away!

"I shall just have to run away," Lan-may thought.

So she took the fish up quickly and holding it fast she began running along the river's edge upstream in the direction in which Alice had gone.

Whom should she meet in a moment but Alice, running along the bank, her bare legs twinkling in the sunshine and her yellow hair flying in the wind?

"Oh, Lan-may!" Alice cried.

"Oh, Alice!" Lan-may cried.

"Lan-may," Alice panted, "I must tell you, my brothers were awful! Lan-may, I couldn't help it."

"What couldn't you help?" Lan-may asked.

"I—I told," Alice gasped. "When I got back my father said where have you been and Tom said she's been outside the gate and my father said I thought I told you not to go outside, and Jack said she's always going outside and I said no, just this once. I went to see if the big net down the river had a fish. We can see your net, Lan-may, from our new house."

"Your new house?" Lan-may repeated.

"We've just moved here," Alice said, "from across the river. Hadn't you heard?"

"No one talks to me," Lan-may said. "My mother never talks because she is a quiet woman, and my father talks only to my brothers because I am a girl, and my brothers talk to one another."

"My father is going to teach English in the school in the city," Alice said. "But my mother said, oh, I can't live in those streets, so we moved out to the edge of the river, and I can see your net from my window. And then my father said was there a fish and I had to say yes, and, oh, Lan-may, before I knew it I had told!"

"So did I," Lan-may confessed, "and now my father is coming to get the dragon fish." She put out her right hand that held the fish. "Sister, we must run away," she said solemnly.

"Yes, Sister, we must," Alice agreed solemnly.

They clasped hands, and Lan-may held the fish tightly in her other hand and they began to run away as fast as they could.

"Where shall we run away to?" Alice asked.

"If we go to the hills there may be tigers in them," Lan-may said without stopping. "We had better go to the city. I think we could sell this fish in the city and get some money to rent a little house where we could live together."

"That would be lovely," Alice said.

They ran toward the city but it was a long way and so at last they had to walk a while to rest.

"Let me carry the dragon fish," Alice said. So Lan-may gave it to her. "It makes my hand feel quite cool," Alice said.

"It did mine, too," Lan-may answered.

It was a lovely afternoon and they felt quite happy. Lan-may had many things to talk about.

"Why is your hair yellow?" she asked Alice. "Is it because your mother ate eggs before you were born?"

Alice laughed. "I don't think so," she said, "because her hair is yellow, too."

"Maybe you all eat eggs," Lan-may said.

"We do eat a lot of eggs," Alice said, "I eat one every day for my supper."

"Do you?" Lan-may exclaimed. "Now, I eat rice and cabbage for mine, and you see how black my hair is."

"It is very black," Alice agreed.

But Lan-may still wanted to talk. It was so nice to have a sister to talk with, somebody who wanted to walk quietly along and just talk without playing at robbers and guerrillas and all such things.

"You speak in a funny way," she told Alice, "why is that?"

"It is because I am an American," Alice said.

At this Lan-may was truly astonished. "How can I understand you, then?" she asked. She was even a little frightened that she could understand an American girl.

Alice laughed. "Because I am speaking Chinese, silly!" she said.

"Can you speak American, too?" Lan-may asked.

"Certainly I can," Alice said and she said something

quickly, something full of ss-ss-sss and kk-kk-kk.

"I can't understand that," Lan-may said.

"That's because you haven't learned it," Alice said.

"Can we be real sisters, though, now that you are American?" Lan-may asked doubtfully.

"Why not?" Alice said. "We really look the same, don't we? Put up your hand, Lan-may."

Lan-may put up her hand and Alice put up hers. "Just the same," she said, "except yours is browner than mine and mine is pinker than yours. But we have

five fingers on each hand. And do you have five toes on each foot?"

"Certainly," Lan-may said.

"And we both have white teeth and our hair is the same stuff, really. I don't mind your hair being black, Lan-may, if you don't mind mine being yellow."

"I tell you what," Lan-may said. "Let's pretend your hair *is* black."

But Alice looked doubtful. "I shouldn't want my hair to be black all the time," she said, "I don't believe my mother would like that."

"I tell you what," Lan-may said, "let's pretend that one day your hair is black and the next day that my hair is yellow."

"All right," Alice said, "and I don't mind mine being black today."

"Thank you, Sister," Lan-may said politely.

So they walked along all through the lovely afternoon until they saw the big city gate ahead of them. Plenty of people looked at them and some people laughed. "Look at the little foreign devil and the little Chinese devil walking together," a man said who was selling peanuts at a corner.

"We don't care, Sister, do we?" Alice said.

"We don't care, Sister," Lan-may replied.

At last they came into the city gate. Lan-may had been there many times when her father brought her with him on holidays and market days and so now she was not at all frightened.

"There is a pawnshop inside the city gate," she told

Alice. "That is so poor country people don't have to walk a long way to pawn their winter coats."

"Do they pawn their winter coats?" Alice asked.

"In the spring," Lan-may told her, "they pawn their winter coats and buy seed, and in the autumn when they have the harvest they take their coats out again. Here is the pawnshop. Give me the fish, Sister."

"Here it is, Sister," Alice said, and gave it to her.

They turned in to a small dark shop and went in, still hand in hand. A little old withered man with a small tight face stood behind the counter.

"Well!" he said, "it is going to rain!"

This is said for a joke, because whenever it is going to rain people say the devils come out, and he saw Alice. But Lan-may did not like it at all. "This is my sister," she said, "and she is not a devil."

"Excuse me," the pawnshop keeper said, smiling a wrinkled smile. "If I had known she was your sister I wouldn't have made such a poor joke."

"I don't mind your calling me a foreign devil," Alice said calmly, "because you don't know any better."

The little old man stared at her and opened his mouth and laughed loudly. "How well you speak Chinese," he said with admiration. "I was entirely mistaken about you."

By now they were all very friendly and so Lan-may put the dragon fish on the counter. There it lay, as heavy as ever, and very still.

"Ha, what is this?" the pawnshop keeper cried. He put on a pair of very large spectacles and took the dragon fish in both hands by its head and tail. "This is a very remarkable fish," he exclaimed. "I have never seen one like it."

"We caught it today while we were fishing in the river, my sister and I," Lan-may said. "We would like to pawn it for enough money to rent a house for us to live in together."

"Alone?" the pawnshop keeper inquired much astonished. "You are very young to live alone."

"We are tired of our brothers," Alice explained, "and so we have left home."

"Ah," the pawnshop keeper said. "I can quite understand that. When I was small I had four sisters and I grew very tired of them. I am still so tired of them that I never go to see them. Now, how would it be if you rented my house? Then you could tend the shop while I go to the tea house and smoke my pipe and drink tea and talk to my friends."

Lan-may and Alice looked at one another. "Would you like to have a shop?" Lan-may asked Alice.

"It might be fun," Alice replied.

All this time they stood hand in hand.

"Let's do it," Lan-may said.

"Let's," Alice replied.

"Very well," the old man said. "Now is a good time to begin. You tend the shop for me while I go to drink tea. By the way, are you hungry?"

"A little," Lan-may said politely.

"Quite a lot," Alice said, not politely at all.

"Let me lock this dragon fish into the glass case," the old man said, "and then I will bring you some small cakes." He locked the fish into the case, first putting it into a big seashell where it looked quite beautiful against the pearly inside. "Now," he said, "we will

38

leave it there until you have lived here long enough for the rent to be used up, and then we will see. Perhaps you can catch another one!" He chuckled a little, and went out to fetch the cakes and brought them in. Then taking up his brass-ended bamboo pipe, he bowed and went away. Inside himself he was much excited. Never had he seen a dragon fish before. The nearest he had come to it was his cousin who knew a man who said he had once seen one.

"I must think of a way to keep this dragon fish," he thought. "Then I shall always have good luck in my shop. Oh, if I could only have this fish for a reward for finding two runaway little girls! Of course their fathers and mothers *will* want to give me a reward?"

While he was worrying about this, Lan-may and Alice were as happy as possible in his shop.

"Isn't this fun?" Alice said. "We won't be bothered any more with brothers!"

"Never!" Lan-may said. "Did your brothers always want to play robbers?"

"They wanted to play robbers all day long," Alice said, "and I always had to be the robbed one."

"So did I," Lan-may said. "And did they always make spears and things?"

"Spears and guns and swords," Alice said, "and they

40

were always pretending I was the enemy."

"So were mine," Lan-may said.

"And they kept saying: 'You're only a girl'."

"So did mine," Lan-may said, "and they said I was a little puss cat."

"Mine called me sissy," Alice said.

"Mine called me afraid-of-her-shadow."

"Mine called me 'fraidy, too," Alice said.

"But we're really very brave," Lan-may said.

"We truly are," Alice agreed.

Lan-may said gaily, "Let's not think about them."

Then they happily began to keep shop. It was really lots of fun. First a woman came in with a ragged scarf she wanted to pawn and they gave her two dollars out of the cash drawer for it, because that was what she asked. She seemed quite surprised and hurried away as though she were afraid that they would take the money away from her. Then came in a man with an old book, and he wanted a dollar for it and so they gave it to him, and after a while another woman came with a baby dress and a tiny pair of shoes and she cried bitterly because she said her baby was dead and she did not want to sell these things but she needed the money to buy food for her other two children. She looked so poor that they gave her two dollars, too.

Then no one came in for a while and they could look around the shop to see what it really was like. It was a very nice little place. Behind the front room were two small bedrooms, and a little kitchen with a clean whitewashed earthen stove. Inside a cupboard was a bowl of pork and chestnuts and a dish of cold rice. These looked so good that they could not bear to shut the cupboard door again. At last Lan-may said, "Do you think it would be wicked to eat?"

"Not wicked," Alice said. "We could tell him we were still hungry."

So Lan-may put some grass into the stove under the small cauldron, and she lit the grass with matches that lay on a ledge, and Alice put the rice into one side of the cauldron and the pork and chestnuts into the other and in a few minutes the food was hot and they put it into bowls and ate it rather quickly, because after all it would be embarrassing if the old man came back.

"Do you think he has something else for supper?" Alice asked.

"If he hasn't," Lan-may said, "he could step across the street and buy some dumplings from the bake shop there. My father and I quite often buy dumplings when we come into the city."

"But the money?" Alice asked.

"We will tell him to count it off the dragon fish," Lan-may said.

So they felt quite happy again and they went back into the shop and looked at the little fish.

"How lucky that we found him," Lan-may said.

"First he brought us together," Alice said, "and second we found this nice little shop. What if the old man never comes back? Perhaps he has run away too."

"I don't care," Lan-may said. "We'll just keep on living in this nice shop." And they began to look at all the things in it while they waited for somebody to come in. There were all sorts of things, old watches and clocks, old knives and chopsticks and dishes and quilts and books and snuff bottles and vases and incense urns and paintings and old brass scales for weighing things, and rings and earrings, pipes of all kinds, and old shoes and pillows and embroidered caps and jackets and from the ceiling there hung old pots and copper vessels and tea kettles. But nothing was as beautiful as the green dragon fish lying in his pearly shell.

By the time they had looked at everything, the end of the day had come and the old man had not come back, and nobody came in except two boys with an old tin can. "We don't want your old tin can," Alice said to the boys.

"Certainly we don't," Lan-may agreed.

So the two boys could only go away again and still the old man did not come back. It was growing near the end of the day. The sun had set and the streets outside the shop were dim with twilight.

"Perhaps he never will come back," Lan-may said.

Not for anything would she have told Alice, but she was getting just a little afraid. She had never been in the city at night before, and she knew that the great gate in the wall would be locked fast and no one could come in or go out. She fetched the matches and lit a candle in a tall pewter stand and it threw flickering shadows on the walls.

And though Alice would never have told Lan-may, she, too, was a little afraid. After all, she was the only yellow-haired blue-eyed child in this whole city, and she felt the beginnings of being lonely.

"I wish the old man would come back," Lan-may said at last.

"Why?" Alice asked.

"Oh, just because," Lan-may said.

"I wish he would, too," Alice said.

"I wonder what my brothers are doing without me," Lan-may said after a while.

"I can't imagine what mine are doing without me,"

Alice said after another while.

"They can't be playing robbers, because they haven't anybody to be robbed now that we are not there," Lan-may said.

"And they can't be playing soldiers because who would be the enemy?" Alice said.

"I didn't mind being robbed sometimes," Lan-may said after another while. "It was only that I didn't want all the time to have to be robbed."

"And I didn't mind being the enemy sometimes," Alice said, "it was just that I got tired of being shot at all the time and having to play dead every single day."

They sat down side by side on a bench and clasped hands again. But neither of them told the other that she was beginning to feel lonely. The little shop was so very quiet. Outside the windows the streets were growing really dark, and people were beginning to light lamps and candles. Through the wide-open doors Alice and Lan-may could see the families laughing and talking, and the children playing, but they only went on sitting on the bench and holding hands and feeling just a little more lonely all the time.

As for the old man, he had gone straight to the teashop and he was still sitting there. He was waiting, too. He was waiting for somebody to come to the teashop and call out, "Has anybody seen two runaway little girls? One is foreign and one is Chinese. They ran away from home this afternoon, carrying a green dragon fish. Anybody seeing the runaways please report to the police station and receive a reward."

It was getting late but he was perfectly sure that if he waited long enough he would hear somebody call. Then he would get up and say, "I know where the two little girls are." Then they would say, "What shall we give you for a reward?" "Please, just the dragon fish," he would say. He would sell this fish for a lot of money. With the money he would buy himself a new black satin jacket and plum-colored satin robe and a new tobacco pipe with a silver bowl and mouthpiece and he would also buy a dish of the best sharks' fin soup.

"I'll just wait," he said. "I'll just wait."

Now anybody can imagine what was going on in Lan-may's home and in Alice's too. Indeed, exactly the same sort of thing was going on in both homes. The two mothers were crying, Mrs. Wu quietly because she was a quiet woman, and Alice's mother, whose name was Mrs. Jones, was crying too, but not quietly. She was crying quite loudly and she was talking all the time she was crying. She was talking to Mr. Jones and to Tom and Jack.

"I tell you we just have to find Alice right away," she was sobbing. "I shan't eat or sleep until we know where she is. And let me tell you all that when she comes home again you have to be nicer to her. The poor little thing—Tom and Jack, you are very naughty to your sister. You are always teasing her and—and she was telling me only the other day that she had to be the enemy all the time—and I remember, the poor darling, that she said she wished she had a sister—that she was so tired of being the only girl and having her brothers always—always—"

"My dear," Mr. Jones said, "please control yourself. We will find her."

"Mr. Jones," Mrs. Jones said, crying more than ever, "you don't understand women and you never have. If we don't find our precious Alice—"

"We *will* find her," Mr. Jones said a little more loudly. "The police are out everywhere—"

"Why don't *you* go?" Mrs. Jones sobbed, "you and Tom and Jack!"

"We *are* going," Mr. Jones said. "I only stayed to try to help you."

"Oh, go—go—go, all of you!" Mrs. Jones cried, and the tears ran down her cheeks in two little rivers. "I am so tired of all of you! Just wait until Alice comes home and if ever you don't treat her right again—oh, darling Alice, where are you—"

But Mr. Jones and Tom and Jack had already gone and when Mrs. Jones saw this she stopped crying and wiped her cheeks and went into Alice's little room and turned down the sheets and got out a clean pair of pajamas, and then she went into the kitchen and toasted bread and warmed milk and put out an egg all ready for Alice's supper.

"Poor Alice," she thought, "she *shall* have a sister— just as soon as she comes back I'll go out and find a little girl—I don't care how much trouble it is."

And then because she couldn't think of anything else to do she went and got two clean handkerchiefs from her top drawer and sat down in the rocking chair and began crying again.

As for Mrs. Wu, she simply had gone on crying steadily and not saying a word until Mr. Wu lost his temper. "Will you stop crying?" he said. "I feel as though the whole house were damp with your tears. Lan-may will be found—why, who wants a girl? Nobody is going to steal a girl. She has wandered away somewhere. We have the police hunting everywhere. It is only a matter of time. Please stop crying, I say!"

Mrs. Wu was sitting on a little bamboo stool and she

went on crying as though she heard not one word of all this. Mr. Wu turned to his sons. "Can you three dolts say nothing to comfort your mother?" he demanded.

At this Mrs. Wu lifted her head, "No," she said, "they cannot. It's their fault our Lan-may ran away."

"Now," said Mr. Wu to the boys, "what did you do?"

"Lan-may was so tired of them," Mrs. Wu said. "You were all so—so mean to her!"

Never had she spoken so many words. Mr. Wu was stunned. "Mean to Lan-may?" he asked. His voice sounded quite weak.

"Yes, you were," Mrs. Wu said, "because she was only a girl."

And she began to cry again. She cried and she cried until the front of her coat was wet and until Mr. Wu did really not know what to do with her.

"I can't stand any more of this," he said at last to Sheng, Tsan, and Yung. "You boys come with me. We will go out ourselves and find Lan-may and bring her home and when we find her I shall spank her for upsetting her mother."

At this moment Mrs. Wu lifted her head and stopped crying long enough to say just a few more words. "Oh, go on—I *am* tired of you all!" she said.

And she began to cry again.

Thus it happened that while Lan-may and Alice were sitting on the bench in the little pawnshop, hand in hand, thinking about their brothers and their mothers and fathers, being more and more lonely, their homes were all in an upset. Quite separately Mr. Jones and Tom and Jack and Mr. Wu and Sheng, Tsan, and Yung were going to the city to find out what the police had done, and indeed find out whatever they could. They did not know one another, of course, and they had no idea that their two girls were sisters.

Separately they came to the city gate just as the guard was thinking about closing it for the night, and Mr. Jones got there first because his legs were longer than Mr. Wu's. He put up his hand to the guard. "Wait," he said, "don't shut the gate. I don't suppose you have seen a runaway girl, about so high, yellow hair, blue eyes?"

"I haven't," the guard said, "but then I sleep most of the afternoon and anything could come through the gate for all of me."

"What shall I do?" Mr. Jones said helplessly. "I am a stranger in the city—I'm the new English teacher at

the school. I don't know anybody and my wife is crying her eyes out."

The guard scratched his bristly head, and looked kind. "My advice," he said to Mr. Jones, "is to go to the teashop and ask in a loud voice if anybody has seen your daughter."

"Thank you," said Mr. Jones.

So Mr. Jones went on and with him went Tom and Jack, who all this time had said nothing.

Mr. Wu followed only two minutes later. He put up his hand to the guard, who now was really considering whether he should not lock the gate for the night. "Wait," said Mr. Wu. "Have you seen a runaway girl about so high?"

"Yellow hair and blue eyes?" the guard asked.

"Certainly not," Mr. Wu said indignantly. "What do you think I am—a foreign devil?"

"Well, the last time it was a foreign devil that asked about a runaway girl. He measured off just so high, too, and he had sons with him, too."

"It's the day of runaway girls," Mr. Wu exclaimed.

"My advice," said the guard, "is to go to the teashop and announce the matter and ask if anybody has seen your daughter."

"Thank you," said Mr. Wu, "I should have thought

of that for myself."

So he hurried away and with him went Sheng, Tsan, and Yung and all this time the three boys said not one word.

Meanwhile the old pawnshop keeper, having drunk so much tea that he felt as though he were a barrel of tea, and having waited until he was tired, was just about to go, when Mr. Jones came into the shop and with him his sons.

"Ah," said the old pawnshop keeper, "now here they are!"

But before Mr. Jones could speak Mr. Wu burst in and with him his three sons, and Mr. Wu began at once to call out.

"Has anybody seen a runaway girl about so high, black hair, black eyes—"

"Also a yellow-haired, blue-eyed girl about so high!" Mr. Jones called out immediately after him.

The teashop was full of men who were talking over their business or playing games of checkers and chess or else just sitting peacefully and smoking.

"Was there also a green dragon fish?" the old pawnshop keeper called back.

By now everybody was looking up surprised. Only one pair of old men kept on playing chess as though

nothing were happening.

"Your move," one old man said.

The other old man moved an ivory piece. "Your move," he murmured in turn.

Mr. Jones looked puzzled. "Green fish?" he repeated. He did not speak Chinese very well, being an American, and he wondered if he had heard wrongly—"fish or dish?" he asked. "Fish, dish or wish or—or—"

"Fish," Mr. Wu said firmly. "There was a green fish, I remember—but was it a dragon fish?"

Mr. Jones looked at him in astonishment. "Do you know about this?" he asked.

"No," Mr. Wu said, "not really. At least—"

By now the old pawnshop keeper was moving briskly through the crowd. Everybody was excited. "Two runaway girls and a runaway fish," they were asking. Only the two old men playing chess did not look up. "Your move," one murmured.

The other one moved a little ivory piece. "Your move," he said.

Now the pawnshop keeper was walking quickly down the street. On one side of him was Mr. Jones and on the other side was Mr. Wu. Behind were all the brothers. "I have had many strange things come into

57

my shop," the pawnshop keeper was saying, "but nothing as strange as your two daughters and the green dragon fish. They told me that they were tired of their brothers and had run away."

"Tired of their brothers?" Mr. Jones exclaimed.

"Tired of their brothers?" Mr. Wu cried.

"And so they ran away together, with the green dragon fish, which they found in the river," the old man said. "I understood them entirely, for in my youth I was tired too, but of my four sisters. I am still tired of them. So I took the two girls into my shop and put the fish into my locked glass case in a seashell, and I told them to wait. I knew that the girls would not go away without the fish, and I did not give them the key to the case, and so doubtless they are there still."

There they were indeed. By now Alice and Lan-may were very homesick indeed, and they were even quite ready to be the enemy and the robbed but what could they do? While they were waiting the guard had really shut the gate, and they had just begun to cry when the door opened, and in came the old pawnshop keeper, Mr. Jones, Mr. Wu, and all their brothers. And all this time the brothers had not said anything.

"Now then, Lan-may," Mr. Wu said sternly.

"Now then, Alice," said Mr. Jones, also sternly.

But the two fathers could not go on being stern, for the two little girls flung themselves into their fathers' arms.

"Please take us home!" they sobbed.

"It is very annoying," Mr. Wu said, with his arms around Lan-may, "but we shall have to pay the guard to open the gate."

"Never mind," Mr. Jones said, with his arms around Alice, "it will be worth it to get our little girls home."

They were all about to go when the pawn-shop keeper said in a trembling voice, "What about the fish, please?"

At this they stopped. "Where is this wonderful fish?" Mr. Wu asked.

"Here," said the pawnshop keeper faintly, and he unlocked the case very slowly for fear they would take it away, too. There the green dragon fish lay, heavy and quiet in the shell.

"You keep it," Mr. Wu said politely, "as your reward."

The pawnshop keeper was delighted. His face crackled into smiles. "Thank you," he said, "I call it a good day's business."

He bowed them away, put up the boards to his shop, and then he went into his kitchen. He was a little surprised to see his supper all gone, but the dishes were neatly washed, and he was good about it. "Never mind," he thought, "I am really too full of tea," and he took off his shoes and his coat and laid himself down in his bed and went to sleep.

As for Alice and Lan-may, they told their fathers everything and by the time they got home they were sleepy and tired indeed. Mr. Jones turned Alice over to Mrs. Jones who of course stopped crying at once. She bathed Alice and fed her toast and warm milk and a poached egg.

It was while she was eating the egg that Alice remembered something. "Mother," she said, "is it because I eat so many eggs that my hair is yellow?"

"Certainly not. I never heard of such a thing," Mrs.

Jones said. "Who told you that?"

"Lan-may," Alice said.

And Mr. Wu turned Lan-may over to Mrs. Wu who stopped crying at once and washed Lan-may all over and fed her hot rice and cabbage soup.

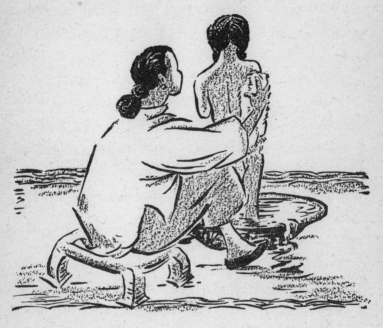

"Mother," Lan-may said, "is it because I don't eat enough eggs that my hair is black?"

"Certainly not," said Mrs. Wu, "who told you that?"

"Alice," Lan-may said.

Outside the Jones house Mr. Jones was saying to

Tom and Jack in a stern voice, "I don't want you to tease your sister any more, do you hear me? No more making her be the enemy all the time, and always making her the seek in hide and seek!"

"We won't," they promised. "Ever!" they added.

And outside the Wu house Mr. Wu was saying firmly to Sheng and Tsan and Yung, "You are not to make your sister be the enemy all the time and the robbed—do you hear me?"

"We won't," they promised. "Ever!"

"Mother," Alice said sleepily when she was all tucked in her bed. "May I play with Lan-may tomorrow?"

"Certainly you may," Mrs. Jones said.

"Every day?" Alice asked.

"Every day," Mrs. Jones promised.

And in her little bamboo bed while her mother tucked her quilt around her Lan-may was saying sleepily, "Tomorrow I am going to play with my sister Alice, and the next day and the next day. Mother, may I play with her every day?"

"Why not?" Mrs. Wu said. "Of course you may."

She blew out the candle and Lan-may lay awake for one half of one minute, just long enough to remember the dragon fish.

"It did bring me luck," she thought, "because now I have a sister."

And then she fell asleep.